DOCTOR·WHO

DECIDE YOUR DESTINY

BBC CHILDREN'S BOOKS
Published by the Penguin Group
Penguin Books Ltd, 80 Strand, London, WC2R 0RL, England
Penguin Group (USA) Inc., 375 Hudson Street, New York, New York 10014, USA
Penguin Books (Australia) Ltd, 250 Camberwell Road, Camberwell, Victoria 3124, Australia
(A division of Pearson Australia Group Pty Ltd)
Canada, India, New Zealand, South Africa
Published by BBC Children's Books, 2007
This edition produced for The Book People Ltd, Hall Wood Avenue, Haydock, St Helens. WA11 9UL.
Text and design © Children's Character Books, 2007
Written by Colin Brake
10 9 8 7 6 5 4 3 2 1
ISBN-13: 978-1-85613-141-4
ISBN-10: 1-85613-141-6
Printed in Great Britain by Clays Ltd, St Ives plc

DOCTOR·WHO

DECIDE YOUR DESTINY

The Haunted Wagon Train

by Colin Brake

The Haunted Wagon Train

1 | The Doctor has promised you a trip into history. 'Just the one trip, remember,' he tells you.

'As long as you do, Doctor,' adds Martha sharply. 'He tends to get a bit distracted,' she explains to you with a kindly smile. 'He offered me "just one trip" and I ended up going back and forth in time like a yo-yo before he eventually got me home.'

'But it was just a day after you'd left, Martha, be fair,' complains the Doctor, turning to adjust a control.

You repeat that you're happy — and grateful — to be offered even the one trip and that you'll be perfectly happy to be taken straight home afterwards.

'There you are then, no problem,' the Doctor says, glancing at Martha as if to say, 'OK?'

'It's only right and proper, though,' Martha agrees, 'after you helped us out with those essential supplies we needed. Are you sure you won't get into trouble for letting us have that old thermometer?'

'No, it was meant to be going to the dump, but because of the mercury we weren't sure if we could just throw it away.'

'Quite right,' the Doctor tells you, 'you can't get rid of a heavy metal like that. Especially when it's so useful. It's essential to certain TARDIS functions...'

'Mercury! How high-tech is that?' says Martha scornfully.

'You'd be surprised at the ways all sorts of common elements can be used in even the most complex technologies,' the Doctor tells you both. 'I've seen star ships powered by coal, grass, even gold!'

Before he can go any further a light begins flashing on the console, accompanied by a beep.

If the instruments show a time distortion, go to 16. If the instruments show a peculiar energy reading, go to 46.

2 To your horror the Doctor nods his head in agreement. 'Of course, that's very wise of you. Martha, perhaps you and our young friend here can take a little look around?'

'I'm sure someone will happily share some food with you,' adds the Captain. 'Tell people that you're a guest of mine.'

Martha looks as if she is about to argue but the Doctor fixes her with a stern look. 'Off you go, Miss Jones,' he tells her, 'I'm sure you'll see and hear lots of interesting things.'

You and Martha move off to take a look around. 'That's the trouble with time travel,' she mutters, 'you have to put up with a lot of old-fashioned ideas about a woman's place!'

You pass a family sitting around a campfire and a woman calls across to you.

If you answer the woman, go to 51.
If Martha responds first, go to 33.

3 | 'This wagon train is haunted,' says Patience, in a firm voice.

'Patience, that's enough,' her father interrupts abruptly.

'But Pa!' she begins to respond and then, seeing the stern look on her father's face, she stops.

'These good folk don't want to hear any of your foolishness, girl,' Jake Robinson tells her in a more kindly tone.

'Yes, Pa,' says Patience, looking down at the ground.

'I'm sure it's easy to let your imagination run away with you when you're travelling to new places every day,' comments Martha. You notice Mrs Robinson flashing a sharp look in the direction of her husband and wonder what is really going on. Can Patience have been telling the truth? Is the wagon train haunted? Or is there something else going on here?

If the first person you met was Running Bear, go to 25. If the first person you met was Lieutenant Harvard, go to 53.

'Let me help you,' suggests the Doctor.

'Help me change history?' says the alien, confused.

'I meant, let me help you get home,' says the Doctor. 'Your ship needs gold to power its engines, right?' The alien nods. 'Then I'll give you the gold you need.'

Both you and Martha look at the Doctor in amazement. 'Are you telling me you've got a shed load of gold in the TARDIS?' asks Martha.

The Doctor smiles. 'Oh I've got all sorts of things in the old girl. Terrible hoarder me, always picking things up on my travels. There's a room full of hotel soaps somewhere.' Martha raises a suspicious eyebrow. 'No really,' insists the Doctor, 'it is very, very big. You've only seen the tip of the iceberg.'

You soon realise what the Doctor meant. The journey through the TARDIS takes ages, and dragging a heavy cart of gold back through the many corridors of the space/time craft takes even longer but, finally, you get back to the console room.

A little later the Doctor dematerialises the TARDIS and lands close to the place where the alien's ship has been hidden and the necessary refuelling takes place.

'I would have tried not to change history,' the alien tells

you, 'I was just going to try and find the gold I needed and leave history to take its course.'

'Word would have got out though,' suggests Martha, 'as soon as you hit the first seam of gold.'

'And that's not due to happen for another five years,' the Doctor reminds him.

The alien thanks you again and, a moment later, the spaceship takes off.

'Will this stop all the weird things going on at the wagon train?' you ask.

If the Doctor answers 'yes', go to 97. If he's not sure, go to 31.

5 The explosion rocks you all off your feet. Smoke and dust fill the air and for a moment it is impossible to see anything. When the airborne debris begins to clear, you see that the entrance to the cave has been completely sealed.

'Doctor!' you cry out in horror and begin trying to pull at the rocks and boulders that now block the entrance.

'It's no good,' Martha tells you, pulling you clear. 'You'll never get through that way.'

'But the Doctor...' you begin and then trail off as you see the determination on Martha's face.

'Wouldn't want us to start getting morbid prematurely,' she says, finishing your sentence.

The scout – Nathaniel McDermott – gets to his feet.

'There's another exit from that cave,' he tells you, 'follow me and I'll show you.'

If you agree to follow him, go to 96. If you are not sure about following him, go to 90.

6 Suddenly the sky is full of fast-moving coloured lights, streaking above your heads. The clouds in the sky reflect the colours — red, yellow and blue. It looks like a special effect at a rock concert.

And then, as suddenly as they appeared, they all disappear, leaving the night sky dark again.

'What was that?' gasps Martha.

'Something alien,' says the Doctor, 'and we need to find out exactly what.'

'How are we going to do that?' you ask, but the Doctor has already pulled his sonic screwdriver from his pocket and is using it to track the energy trail left by the lights.

The trail leads to a wagon parked just inside the circle. There is no campfire next to it, and no sign of life. 'Let's take a look inside,' suggests the Doctor.

If Martha goes in first, go to 41. If the Doctor goes first, go to 10.

7 One of the older boys is teasing the others. 'Make sure you stay in your beds tonight. Or you'll get taken to the Ghost Train!' The younger children squeal and scream and run away back to their parents. The boy laughs.

'That wasn't very nice,' comments Martha and makes the boy jump.

'I didn't mean no harm, Miss,' he stammers, 'it was just a joke.'

'The little ones didn't seem to think it was very funny,' you point out.

The boy looks sheepish but another lad sticks up for him.

'Jimmy was just telling the truth,' he tells you. 'There is a ghost train, there is!'

The boys run off as the Doctor rejoins you.

'You've been hearing about the ghost train too?' he asks.

You both nod.

> **If the Doctor leads you out of the camp, go to 48. If the Doctor leads you into the middle of the camp, go to 12.**

8 | Martha leads the way through the tall grass. 'Be careful,' she warns you, 'there might be snakes in the grass.'

'Do you have to be so cheerful?' you ask her, keeping your eyes firmly looking downwards.

'Sorry,' she replies, 'but travelling with the Doctor is not always a picnic. In fact,' she adds after a moment's thought, 'it's never a picnic.'

'Maybe we can insist on a picnic next trip,' you suggest.

'If we don't find the Doctor there won't be another trip,' she reminds you.

The trail is leading you out of the tall grass and on to rocky hills.

'How did someone from the nineteenth century get hold of technology like that weapon?' you wonder.

'Good question,' Martha agrees.

Suddenly she comes to a stop.

If you've been following the trail of a Native American, go to 85. If not, go to 42.

9 Lieutenant Harvard stands before you. 'I knew you three were going to be trouble,' he mutters.

'Trouble? Us?' says the Doctor, sounding hurt, 'we never trouble anyone,' he assures the shape-shifter, 'unless they trouble us.' He concludes in a more threatening tone of voice.

The fake lieutenant looks around nervously. 'So who are you? Imperial Guards? Time Agents?'

'Actually you'd be better off thinking of us as the galactic AA,' says the Doctor, 'only we don't have the uniforms and you don't have to join a club. But we're here to help, if you want our help, and I suspect you do, 'cos this is a time machine isn't it? Primitive, crude even, but it got you here, didn't it?'

The man nods, stunned into silence.

'So why haven't you moved on? Why join a wagon train under cover?'

If the alien answers, go to 22. If he changes shape, go to 49.

10 The Doctor leads the way into the wagon and gestures for you and Martha to stay back.

'Come on,' Martha whispers to you, 'we don't want to miss anything do we?'

She scrambles into the wagon and you follow her.

As soon as you step inside you can feel a peculiar atmosphere. At first you cannot put your finger on what it is that is so odd and then it hits you — there is a soft electrical hum in the background, a bit like the sound you hear in the TARDIS control room. But there's no sign of any machinery, or the Doctor come to that.

Martha spots that heavy drapes separate the entrance area from the rest of the wagon and she pulls them aside.

'Ah, there you are,' says the Doctor, who you can now see beyond the drapes.

If he is alone, go to 73. If not, go to 50.

11 In almost every direction you look the view is exactly the same — an endless prairie covered in tall grass wavering gently in the wind. Behind you is a small copse of trees. You glance back at it and can just make out a flash of blue, which must be the TARDIS. As you walk away from it you feel a twinge of fear and apprehension.

Your Native American guide moves with panther-like grace, making no noise as he pushes through the tall grass like a ghost.

'If this is the Wild West of Cowboys and Indians, why is he helping us?' you ask the Doctor in a whisper.

'You've been watching too many Western films,' he tells you. 'The reality was very different to Hollywood's version.'

You realise that your guide has disappeared.

If you can see a trail, go to 59. If you hear a noise, go to 29.

You follow the Doctor back towards the storage wagons in the centre of the camp. When he reaches them, the Doctor begins to clamber up the wagons and manages to get on to the roof of the TARDIS.

'What are you doing?' asks Martha.

'Getting a bit of height,' he tells you. 'This area is so flat, you can see for miles if you can just get high enough.'

You and Martha climb up to join him.

'I hope the TARDIS will take our weight!' you mutter, nervously, as you climb on to the roof.

The Doctor takes some night vision glasses from his pocket and looks out towards the distant horizon.

'Oh, now that's interesting,' he comments.

'What can you see?' asks Martha.

'Another wagon train,' the Doctor tells her. 'No, scrub that. It's actually an exact copy of this wagon train!'

He passes the night vision glasses to you and, when you look through the viewfinder, you can see what he means. In the distance is a perfect copy of the wagon train camp that you are in — it's almost like looking in a mirror. As you take it in, however, the twin begins to disappear.

'It's fading away,' you announce, handing back the glasses.

The Doctor doesn't seem too surprised. 'Phantoms often do,' he tells you, putting the glasses to his eyes again.

'But what was it?'

'I don't know but I know a man who might — there's someone out there on the prairie. Let's go and have a word.'

A few minutes later the Doctor has led you both back through the camp and out into the open, where you find the figure that the Doctor saw approaching you.

If he is dressed in leather and furs, go to 83. If he is dressed in Native American garb, go to 92.

13 | Carefully you move towards the Native American who is holding Martha.

He whispers urgently at you. 'Please listen to me. I won't harm you. If you promise not to make any sound I will release her.'

You look Martha in the eyes. You can see that she looks frightened. 'I think we can trust him,' you tell her in a whisper. 'Okay, let her go.'

The man removes his hand from Martha's mouth and he lets her go. She hurries to your side.

'Your friend — the wise one,' the Native American begins to say.

'You mean the Doctor?' Martha checks, with a little giggle. The man nods and continues.

'He is in trouble. Great danger. But if you keep quiet, I think I can go into the cave and help him.'

You and Martha exchange looks.

If you agree to his plan, go to 93. If you're not sure, go to 35.

14 A few hours later you have 'borrowed' some horses and have left the camp on the trail of the crashed spaceship. Soon you are able to see the ship in the distance — it rises above the horizon to the height of a three-storey house — but as you get a little nearer you see a Native American camp surrounding the organic shell-like ship.

'We could just go and explain who we are and what that is,' suggests Martha as you consider the problem from the cover of some trees. The Doctor shares his night vision glasses with you. Through them you can see the Native Americans dancing around the ship. 'It looks like they really value it,' comments the Doctor. 'I don't think they're going to let us just walk in and take it.'

Through the night vision glasses you see a corral of horses a little distance from the campfires and you have an idea. You whisper your plan to Martha and start creeping around the perimeter of the camp, keeping as low and as quiet as you can. Some of the Native American warriors are just a few metres away as you crawl silently past them in the darkness. It seems to take an age but finally you reach the horses and open the gate. Moments later chaos erupts as the released horses scatter in all directions. Suddenly, something knocks you over and you lose consciousness.

When you wake up you are in the TARDIS and the Doctor is smiling at you. 'That was very brave,' he says. He tells you that your plan worked and the diversion you created allowed Lalioah to get to her ship and go home. 'And now,' he announces, 'it's your turn. Time to go home.'

Your adventure in time and space is over.

THE END

15 | 'Well, let's not get bogged down in the politics of it, shall we?' suggests the Doctor hurriedly. 'The point is that we are here on the orders of the President.'

The Lieutenant nods. 'The wagon train is making camp about two miles from here. If we make a start now we should make the camp by nightfall.' He starts to lead you through the tall prairie grass, away from the trees under which the TARDIS landed.

As you walk, you take the chance to fall into step with the Doctor.

'Where are we then?' you ask him in a whisper.

'Where do you think you are?' he asks you with a twinkle in his eye.

'America, of course,' you tell him, 'sometime in the nineteenth century?'

'Very good,' he tells you, making you feel great.

If it is getting dark, go to 62. If it is still light, go to 39.

The Doctor has produced his dark-rimmed glasses from a pocket and is examining the instruments on the central console.

'Some kind of time distortion,' he mutters. 'I'm going to have to take a closer look.'

With a sudden burst of energy the Doctor dashes around the circular console, pulling levers and adjusting controls.

'So where are we heading now?' Martha asks, when the Doctor completes his course correction.

'Still into the past,' he tells you, 'but not as far as I promised. No dinosaurs I'm afraid,' he adds, apologetically.

The TARDIS lands and the Doctor hurries over to the doors.

'Come on then,' he says and before you can say anything he's left.

You follow Martha out of the TARDIS and find that the Doctor already has company.

If he is with a Native American, go to 61. If he is with a Western scout, go to 26.

17 | You are surprised that Running Bear seems to be able to enter the camp unchallenged. The Doctor sees your confusion.

'You have to get all those Hollywood ideas of Cowboys and Indians out of your head,' he tells you and Martha. 'The reality of the situation was that Native Americans were quite friendly to the new settlers when they first appeared on their land. Traders need customers, after all.'

Running Bear has stopped to talk to a man in a slightly dusty-looking Army uniform.

'Of course, things did get a bit hairy later on,' confesses the Doctor in a whisper. 'Just ask my old mate Custer.'

Running Bear brings the uniformed man over to you and introductions are made. 'I'm Captain George Hamilton,' the man tells you, shaking your hand firmly. He is a big man with bright eyes on a face weathered and aged like old leather. He has a thick black moustache.

'Is this a military operation?' Martha asks.

The Doctor has already explained to Captain Hamilton that you have become separated from your own wagon train and Martha's question makes him raise an eyebrow with suspicion.

'Did your own train not have a Captain?'

Martha isn't sure what to say but the Doctor steps in to spare her blushes.

'Of course, we all elected a Captain before we set off but ours wasn't a military man like yourself.'

'That explains a lot,' comments Captain Hamilton dryly, 'no one trained at West Point would have lost three of his people so carelessly.'

With his usual charm, the Doctor seems to have been accepted by these people and you and Martha are given to a woman called Mrs Robinson to be looked after. The Doctor promises to join you later.

If you want to have a meal, go to 54. If you want to sleep, go to 21.

18 'I've been here three lunar cycles,' the alien explains, 'searching for my ride home. And now, finally, I think I've found it.'

'My ship is part organic,' she explains, 'and it had been infected by a virus. It needed time to fight off the infection and recover but it wasn't strong enough to make a safe landing, so I was forced to eject in a life raft.'

'And you've been searching for it for three months?' asks Martha. The alien nods.

'So what about the ghostly noises and strange lights?' Martha continues. 'Where do they fit in?'

'A necessary distraction for the locals,' the alien answers.

'A cover-up,' explains the Doctor, 'to keep the wagon train from worrying too much about your activities.'

'Will you help me?' asks the alien.

If you are with a Huygovan, go to 40. If the alien called itself Lalioah, go to 14.

'You've got this wrong,' says the alien who has posed as Eagle Claw. 'I'm meant to be capturing him!' He points at the scout, who just laughs.

'Don't even try it,' he suggests, 'it won't work.'

'You must listen to me. This creature is wanted on a dozen worlds, he has robbed millions and hurt hundreds of Federation Citizens. I have a warrant for his arrest.'

He begins to reach for something stuffed into his clothing, but the scout darts forward to grab it from him. He hurls it on to the nearest campfire. To your surprise the scroll of what looks like paper hisses and crackles but does not burn. Instead it jumps out of the flames and lands at the Doctor's feet. He bends to pick it up.

'Flame resistant semi-intelligent plastic,' he explains, scanning it quickly, 'perfect for barbeque invites and legal documents. This appears to be in order,' he adds, looking at the scout with a stern expression, 'you're nicked, my son.'

The scout pulls out a weapon, but the Cheyenne Warriors are too quick for him and a swiftly aimed arrow sends it flying out of his hand. Quickly the Native Americans secure the scout and the Doctor disables his image manipulator to reveal a small furry creature that reminds you of a teddy bear.

After this everything seems to happen very quickly. Eagle Claw — now in his true identity as Galactic Law Enforcement Officer

Gan McDee — secures his prisoner in a stasis tube, collects his belongings and decloaks his hidden spaceship. Within minutes he has gone. 'Right then,' says the Doctor turning to you, 'one trip we said, so it's time to get you home.'

A little while later the TARDIS is spinning through the time/ space vortex, taking you home — your adventure is over.

THE END

20 The Doctor is talking to a man in a military uniform. The Doctor makes some quick introductions.

'This is Captain Hamilton,' he tells you. 'He's the Captain of this wagon train, which is two weeks out of Independence, Missouri.'

The Captain, a handsome man with a well-weathered face and a thick dark moustache, shakes your hand. 'I'm charged with getting these folk safely across the wild lands and past hostile natives,' he explains.

'But it's not the natives that have been giving you problems, is it Captain?' the Doctor asks.

The Captain shoots a quick look at you and Martha and raises an eyebrow at the Doctor.

'I'm not sure this is suitable talk for a lady or a youth,' he says.

If the Doctor agrees with the Captain and asks you to leave them, go to 2. If the Doctor disagrees and insists you stay, go to 38.

21 | Mrs Robinson tells you that there's room in her wagon for you both to get some sleep. 'The children will just have to squeeze over,' she tells you with a laugh.

'How many children do you have?' asks Martha politely.

You reach the wagon and three curious children come out to meet you.

'This is Patience — she's eight,' Mrs Robinson tells you proudly, 'but she acts much older. Courage there is six and that little one hiding behind his big sisters is our boy, Endeavour.'

'We really don't want to put you — or your family — to any trouble,' says Martha.

'It's no trouble, Miss Jones,' Mrs Robinson assures you.

'But Ma,' the eldest child begins, 'haven't you told them about what happens at night?'

Mrs Robinson shakes her head.

'What do you mean?' demands Martha.

If Patience answers, go to 3. If a male voice cuts in, go to 55.

'I'm a Joftli,' the alien explains and changes his appearance again. He now looks like a grey shop window dummy.

'I thought your people were all but extinct,' the Doctor states.

'The same has been said about the Time Lords,' replies the Joftli. The Doctor raises a surprised eyebrow. 'I found your blue box in the woods where I met you earlier. Clearly Time Lord technology.'

'So what's this about?' you demand. 'Is this an invasion or what?'

The alien laughs at the idea. 'No, we just need fuel to get home. Gold. Lots of it. Luckily this wagon train is heading right towards a major source of the metal.'

'But the California Gold Rush won't start for another five years,' the Doctor tells him.

The alien shrugs.

> **If the Doctor tells him that he can't change history, go to 56. If the Doctor has an alternative idea, go to 4.**

'I am Lord Jevart, of the Royal House of Darmounder, from the Astares System,' the monster announces grandly, 'and this is my loyal bodyguard, Korst.'

'The Astares System? You're a long way from home,' comments the Doctor.

'One of our scientists began researching time travel,' continues the creature, 'and he created a device to access the space-time vortex but he lost control of it. The machine disappeared.'

Martha thinks she understands. 'And it came here?'

'Exactly,' the alien answers, 'we've been tracking it across space. It's unstable and dangerous.'

The Doctor looks aghast. 'No wonder we saw a duplicate of the wagon train. All the rules of space time are being shattered. That really was the same wagon train in two places at the same time.'

'So where is this device?' you ask.

If it is in the cave, go to 65. If the creature tells you it is elsewhere, go to 57.

You quickly clamber into the back of the wagon and stick your head inside, but it is too dark to see much. Martha and the Doctor join you and the three of you move fully into the mysterious wagon. A little way in, a heavy curtain spans the width of the interior space. The Doctor ducks behind it. A moment later his voice floats back to you.

'I think you two should come on through,' he tells you.

Martha pulls at the curtain and you both slip through the gap she makes, into the rear compartment of the wagon.

It is immediately clear that this is no ordinary 'prairie schooner'. A background electronic hum reminds you of the TARDIS and with good reason — the wagon is lined with complex technological devices and computers.

If the Doctor is alone, go to 73. If he is not, go to 50.

Filled with curiosity about what Patience said – and what she wasn't allowed to say – you have to wait before you can discuss it with Martha in private.

Eventually, after the children have all gone to bed and the Robinsons are busy with chores, you and Martha find yourselves alone by the campfire.

'What do you think all that ghost business was about?' you ask her, after checking that no one is in earshot.

'I don't know,' Martha tells you, 'but I bet it's got something to do with those readings the Doctor took in the TARDIS.'

'Gold star for Ms Martha Jones,' announces the Doctor suddenly, making you both jump.

'How did you creep up on us like that?' demands Martha, annoyed at herself for reacting so obviously. The Doctor grins.

'Oh, I've been taking a few lessons from the locals,' he tells you. 'And that's not all I've been learning from them,' he adds.

You and Martha both look at him expectantly. He beckons you to your feet and starts walking through the camp. You and Martha scramble to follow him.

'Apparently the nights round here are rather interesting,' he tells you. 'Well, I say round here, but I really mean round this wagon train. Every night when they make camp, wherever they make camp, there are reports of strange lights in the sky and peculiar noises.'

'The ghosts are following the wagon train?' Martha asks, puzzled. 'But don't ghosts tend to haunt places not people?'

'Oooh, another gold star for Ms Jones. On a roll tonight, aren't you?'

'But there's no such thing as ghosts, is there?' you interject, hoping for a gold star for yourself, but before the Doctor can answer...

If strange lights flare, go to 6. If a strange sound is heard, go to 32.

The man standing with the Doctor is dressed in dirty brown leather clothing, decorated with furs and wearing what looks like a cowboy hat. In his hands he holds an old-fashioned rifle but for once the weapon isn't being pointed at the Doctor.

'...and these are my travelling companions,' the Doctor is saying. You notice that he is pocketing what looks like a thin wallet.

'Psychic paper,' Martha whispers. 'I'll explain later.'

'This is Lieutenant John Harvard,' the Doctor tells you. 'He's scouting for a wagon train that's setting up camp a few miles from here.'

You and Martha quickly introduce yourselves.

'You folks got separated from your train?' the scout asks you. Martha nods, nervously.

'But no train's been through here for months,' says the scout, with suspicion.

If the Doctor has an answer to that, go to 47. If Martha answers the man, go to 74.

'I think they went this way,' you tell Martha, pointing towards some grass which looks as if it has been pushed out of place. Martha takes a look but a wind has picked up and all the grass is beginning to sway slightly.

'Quickly then,' she tells you, 'before the trail disappears.'

Martha leads the way into the tall grass and you follow her carefully. 'Are we still going away from the camp?' you ask her after a while.

She nods. 'I think we're getting close to the hills,' she tells you. As the ground begins to rise, the height and density of the grass begins to diminish. Soon you are clambering over exposed rock.

Martha suddenly stops in her tracks.

If the man who took the Doctor was a Native American, go to 85. If the man who took the Doctor was a scout, go to 42.

'You must listen to me,' says the scout, 'Eagle Claw is not who he appears to be.'

The Native American Chief, a man called Red Wolf, comes forward and looks the scout in the eyes.

'Neither are you,' he says levelly.

The Doctor steps forward, 'Chief Red Wolf, son of Great Bear, son of Hunting Moon? I visited your people before. Your grandfather knew me as Star Walker.'

'But that is not possible,' says Chief Red Wolf.

'I walk on the Time Winds as well as between the Stars,' the Doctor tells him earnestly.

Convinced, Red Wolf has the suspect, Eagle Claw, brought before you and the Doctor, turns off his image manipulator. He is revealed as a green-skinned alien humanoid.

He begs the Doctor to be allowed to speak.

If the Doctor allows him to speak, go to 19. If the scout tries to shoot him, go to 71.

'Over there!' you call out, pointing. 'I thought I heard something.'

You all stand still and listen. Something is disturbing the corn, and rumbling towards you.

'It can't be our guide,' Martha points out. 'He wasn't making a sound.'

'Be careful,' warns the Doctor and a moment later a huge beast bursts out of the grass and runs at you.

You get a fleeting image of a huge hairy dark creature and a pair of magnificent sharp horns hurtling towards you like a freight train, and then you're knocked off your feet by a flying rugby tackle.

You roll on the floor and discover that you have been rescued by Running Bear, who has come back for you.

'What was that?' you gasp, a little winded.

'A buffalo,' he tells you. 'Come on, we must hurry.'

If it is getting dark, go to 62. If not, go to 39.

30 | Mrs Robinson takes you to her wagon and introduces you to her family. Her husband is a carpenter and is busy mending a couple of wagon wheels and Mrs Robinson has to finish preparing the meal, so you and Martha are left in the hands of the three Robinson children — Endeavour, who is four, Courage who is six and the oldest girl Patience.

'I'm eight and three quarters,' she tells you proudly.

Martha can't help but laugh at her serious expression. 'What's so funny about that?' the little girl demands, hurt at the laughter.

'Nothing,' Martha assures her. 'I just thought it sounded funny.'

'Well it's not,' Patience tells her firmly, 'and you won't find it funny when the ghosts start to ride.'

'What ghosts?' you ask, not sure if you've heard correctly.

If Patience answers you, go to 3. If a male voice interrupts your conversation, go to 55.

'Who knows?' says the Doctor, with a cheerful grin.

'Come on Doctor, there's no such thing as ghosts,' complains Martha.

'Isn't there? Remember your pal Shakespeare?' asks the Doctor. ' "There are more things in heaven and earth,"' he says, recalling the lines Shakespeare wrote for his character Hamlet.

'No, but really. Surely the phantoms were just a side effect of the aliens scanning for gold. Some kind of feedback?' suggests Martha.

The Doctor gives you a wink. 'If you want,' he says.

Martha sighs, realising that the Doctor is winding her up.

'Right,' says the Doctor turning to look at you, 'one trip we agreed. It's time I got you back home.'

Soon the mysterious space/time craft known as the TARDIS is under way again, hurtling back to twenty-first century Earth. When the doors open you see that you are back where you started. Your adventure is over.

THE END

A shrill electronic scream suddenly fills the air. You cover your ears with your hands but you can't shut out the banshee-like wailing.

Suddenly the noise stops and for a moment there is a deathly silence. Then the camp begins to react to the aural assault: dogs bark, babies cry, children scream.

'What was that?' asks Martha.

The Doctor shakes his head. 'Don't know,' he confesses, 'but it was very, very loud. And whatever it was has no place in mid-nineteenth century America, I can tell you that!'

He pulls out his sonic screwdriver and begins taking readings.

'The source is here in the camp,' he tells you, 'this way.'

He starts moving off, across the central part of the camp towards a large wagon that is parked inside the circle. 'In there,' he announces.

If Martha goes in first, go to 41. If you go first, go to 24.

33 | Martha accepts the woman's offer of some food and you sit down to join her and her family. The woman introduces herself as Mrs Robinson and introduces her husband Tom, a serious-looking man who rarely seems to speak. Mrs Robinson, however, talks enough for the pair of them.

Over a plate of bread and vegetables she warns you to take care after dark. 'Best you turn in when the sun goes down, and stay in your bunks until the dawn,' she tells you.

'Why's that?' you ask, curious.

'So you don't see no ghosts, of course,' the woman tells you matter-of-factly.

'What and miss the show?' comes a new voice, as the Doctor strolls up.

'Come on, you two,' he tells you. 'Let's go and see some ghosts!'

If the Doctor leads you out of the camp, go to 48. If the Doctor leads you into the middle of the camp, go to 12.

34 It is a few hours since the incident in the cave and the scout has brought you to the Cheyenne village. Smoke is rising from numerous teepees but most of the tribe are asleep. You take up a position at the edge of the campsite-like village.

The scout has been explaining the situation.

'He is a fugitive, an escapee from a space prison,' the scout tells you all, 'using an image manipulator to make himself look human.'

'Just as you are?' adds the Doctor, with a knowing smile.

'How can you tell?' the scout asks, surprised.

'There's a limit to the image field,' the Doctor tells him, 'your shadow is the wrong shape.'

'So what's the next step?' asks Martha practically.

Before anyone can answer there is a sudden movement and Native American warriors surround you.

If the Doctor speaks, go to 91. If the scout speaks, go to 28.

35 'I don't know,' you say to Martha, 'we don't know anything about this guy.'

'I am Eagle Claw of the Cheyenne Nation. I am an honourable man. You have my word I help your wise friend.'

'If he's so wise why does he keep getting in these fixes?' mutters Martha, half to herself.

'My people have a saying — the wolf who walks on the thinnest ice will go further than one who takes the safe ground.'

'Oh very deep,' comments Martha. 'I'll remember that and send it in to *Reader's Digest*, she tells him.

'Stay here and stay quiet,' Eagle Claw orders you and sets off for the cave, but moments after he enters there is a massive explosion, sending out a cloud of dust and debris.

When it clears you and Martha hurry into the cave.

If Martha goes first, go to 82. If you go first, go to 44.

36 The new arrival appears to be one of the little girls you saw playing outside earlier, but on second glance you see that she is not human at all.

'Please don't be afraid,' she says, her enlarged pupils making her look like a puppy.

'Why would we be afraid?' asks Martha.

The Doctor provides he answer. 'Because our friend here is a Huygovan, a species feared throughout the universe.'

'We mean no harm,' insists the alien.

'Unfortunately that doesn't make you any less dangerous,' the Doctor responds. 'Huygovan's have evolved a sophisticated natural defence. When they encounter a new species they have glands which react to the new species' DNA and create species-specific fatal viruses,' he explains. 'And that's not easy to say — "species-specific!" ' he adds. 'So how long have you been here?' demands the Doctor.

If the alien answers, go to 18. If an alarm sounds, go to 66.

'**W**hy did you call him that?' you ask.

'The Tenth President of the United States came to office in a rather controversial manner,' the Doctor tells you.

'Like George Bush?' asks Martha.

The Doctor shakes his head. 'No, nothing like that. John Tyler was the first President to inherit the role rather than be elected. His predecessor died rather suddenly, not long after his inauguration, of viral pneumonia. Probably his own fault, he insisted on taking the oath of allegiance in freezing cold weather and wore no overcoat. So the new Vice President, John Tyler, found himself unexpectedly promoted.'

'For some of us,' adds the Lieutenant, 'he should only be Acting President.'

'Hence his nickname, "The Accidency",' says the Doctor.

Convinced now of your identities, the Lieutenant takes you to the wagon train.

If you go first, go to 62. If you let Martha go first, go to 39.

'My companions are quite experienced in the perils of frontier life,' the Doctor tells the Captain. 'They can cope with hearing everything you have to say to me. Come on then, what's been the problem?'

'Ghosts,' the Captain tells you, seriously, 'this wagon train is haunted.'

You and Martha exchange a look. You both know that there is no such thing as ghosts, however to your surprise the Doctor seems to be taking the suggestion at face value.

'Ghosts?' he repeats, nodding. 'And what exactly is it that's haunting you?'

The Captain looks up at the sky, which is getting dark. 'You'll be able to see for yourself soon enough.' He tells you that you should get into a good position to see the phantoms.

If he sends you to the middle of the camp, go to 12. If he sends you out of the camp, go to 48.

Your guide leads you into a valley where the wagon train has made camp for the day.

'Wow!' You can't help being impressed.

'You can say that again,' says Martha, equally struck by the sight before you.

The camp is massive, made up of over 100 large covered wagons, drawn up in a massive circle. Numerous small campfires have been set up inside the perimeter. There are oxen in a temporary enclosure and horses, too.

The sight looks a bit similar to a caravan site or a campsite. You can see some small children playing a game with a stick, while some older kids are feeding the animals.

As you walk into the camp the people you pass regard you with quiet suspicion, their faces dark with weeks of dust and dirt.

If your guide is a native, go to 17. If your guide is a soldier, go to 69.

The Doctor shrugs. 'We have to help,' he states, 'before you wipe out the human race.'

'Please,' the alien insists, 'I mean you no harm. It's my nature.'

The Doctor begins to help the alien pack up her equipment. 'We can't have any of this technology left here,' he comments. Once everything is packed, your party creep out quietly through the camp. You and Martha want to say goodbye to your hosts but the Doctor wants to leave without any fanfare.

Soon you are walking back into the small wood in which the TARDIS landed. When the familiar blue box comes into view you see that someone is waiting for you. It is a Native American.

'Kill him,' the alien child orders. 'Quickly!'

The Doctor raises an eyebrow. 'And what was that you were saying earlier about meaning us no harm?'

'He's just a savage,' spits the alien, furious at the Doctor's failure to obey her order.

'There's only one savage here,' the Doctor tells her with a furious expression on his face. He produces his sonic screwdriver. A high-pitched tone fills the air and everything turns to black...

When you and Martha come round you are in the TARDIS with the Doctor. 'Sorry about that,' he tells you both, 'but I had no choice.'

'Where's the alien?' you ask.

'And that Native American?' adds Martha.

'Gone,' explains the Doctor. 'That Native American was actually another member of the alien's race. Here to take that dangerous young alien home to complete her education and learn how not to be a threat to every creature she meets.'

The Doctor glances at you. 'And talking of home… it's time I got you back where you belong as well…'

The TARDIS materialises in your street and you realise your adventure is over.

THE END

41 Martha pulls herself up and into the wagon. 'Some stairs would have been nice,' she mutters in a whisper.

'Maybe they didn't want visitors,' you whisper back, as she helps you up to join her. The Doctor vaults the distance with ease, landing without a noise on the wooden floor of the wagon.

'Perhaps I'd better go first,' he tells you.

'Do you think it might be dangerous?' you ask, suddenly worried.

The Doctor fixes you with a serious look.

'Something anachronistic is going on here,' he tells you, 'something that doesn't belong in this time zone. We should be cautious. Wait here.'

He steps inside and disappears into the darkness.

You and Martha exchange a nervous look. Suddenly you hear the Doctor asking you to follow him. You pull the heavy curtains aside and enter.

If you find him inside alone, go to 73. If you find that he is not alone, go to 50.

There is a cave mouth in front of you — glowing with an electric blue colour that cannot possibly be from any natural source. 'More high technology?' you whisper to Martha. She nods and suggests that you get a little closer.

Keeping low to the rocky ground you both creep forward towards the cave. As you get closer you can see a familiar figure standing in the entrance to the cave — a dark shadow framed by the blue glow. It is the Doctor and he is addressing someone — or something — deeper inside the cave.

'He must be in there with the scout bloke,' you speculate.

'Let's wait out here and see what happens. He may have a gun on the Doctor or something,' Martha whispers back to you.

'It's okay,' you hear the Doctor's voice float back to you on the night air, 'I don't want to hurt you. Just put down the gun.'

You and Martha exchange a quick look. She was right. The Doctor is being held at gunpoint. 'We have to rescue him,' you suggest.

'None of this equipment belongs here,' the Doctor continues, 'not in this place, or this time. So tell me, who are you and what do you want here?'

'I just want to be left alone,' the stranger yells at the Doctor.

'Yeah, like he's going to do that,' you mutter to yourself, smiling. You glance to the side to see if Martha is amused and realise, with a sudden cold shock, that Martha has gone.

You turn around and see that she is being held by one of the locals. He has one hand clamped over Martha's mouth and a knife in his other hand.

If he releases Martha and runs into the cave, go to 78. If he beckons you to come closer, go to 13.

43 'Running Bear!' you exclaim in amazement.

'That explains a lot,' says the Doctor. 'I thought you accepted our arrival a little too easily. Who did you think we were — Time Agents, Galactic police?'

'Imperial Agents,' says the man calling himself Running Bear. 'I thought you might be agents of the Draconian Empire.'

'And why would Imperial Agents be looking for you?' asks the Doctor, with a hint of suspicion. 'Could it have something to do with the time machine you stole?'

Running Bear is amazed. 'How did you know?'

The Doctor grins. 'Oh, just a lucky guess,' he says with a modest shrug. 'But something's wrong, you're a long way and a long time from home and your time machine isn't working. What's the problem? Why hook up with a wagon train? What are you after?'

If the alien answers, go to 49. If the alien says nothing, go to 22.

44 | A metre or so into the cave a strange sensation comes over you and you feel momentarily faint. You close your eyes and when you open them you are no longer in a cave at all. You appear to be on some sort of spaceship.

You look around and see that the Doctor, the Native American and the scout are all here. You are standing in a small semicircular alcove on one wall. You see Martha next to you, looking as disorientated as you feel.

'You've just been through a matter transporter,' says the Doctor, 'take a few deep breaths and you'll soon feel better.'

'Where are we?' you manage to ask.

'In my ship,' answers the scout, 'in orbit around your planet.'

'You're an alien?'

The scout looks offended. 'I'm as human as you are,'

'But displaced in time?' suggests the Doctor.

The Native American is watching on in awe. 'It is your magic which has been making the phantoms?' he asks.

The scout looks a bit sheepish. 'I'm from the twenty-eighth century. I was on a routine flight and hit some kind of temporal anomaly. Got thrown a thousand years into the past. So I had to send out a mayday.'

'The ghost wagon train was an SOS?!'

The Doctor smiles at you. 'Exactly.'

'You are from the future?' asks the Native American. 'Tell me, does the Cheyenne Nation survive?'

The scout glances at the Doctor and then answers.

'Your land becomes part of the United States of America but your people survive. In fact the eighty-sixth President is one of your people.'

The Doctor interrupts before too much is said. 'Shall we see about getting you home?' he asks.

If the Doctor uses the TARDIS, go to 63.
If he does something with the spaceship, go to 70.

45 An ear-piercing noise suddenly fills the air. You put your hands over your ears but you cannot block the electronic scream out of your head. It makes your whole body shake. Your eyes are squeezed shut. You find yourself falling to the floor and then, as suddenly as it began, it stops.

You open your eyes and see Martha lying in a heap next to you.

'Are you okay?' she asks you.

'I think so,' you tell her, wiping tears from your face. To your relief you see that Martha is doing the same thing.

You look around and realise that your attacker has disappeared.

'He's gone,' you say.

'And so has the Doctor!' Martha realises. 'They must have gone that way,' she suggests, pointing at a trail leading off through the tall grass. 'Let's go!'

If Martha goes first, go to 8. If you go first, go to 86.

The Doctor dashes around the console, checking various read-outs for the cause of the alarm.

'What is it?' you ask, hoping it isn't a problem that is going to end your journey before it has even begun.

The Doctor sighs, 'It's an energy reading, but it's not possible...'

He moves around the central console making quick adjustments to the controls. 'We're going to have a change of plan,' he announces. The TARDIS engines give a final roar and the time/space ship materialises at its new destination.

'So where have we landed now?' Martha asks the Doctor, who hurries over to the external doors.

'Earth,' he tells you before disappearing outside, 'the United States of America to be precise. Mid-nineteenth century!'

You and Martha exchange a look. 'Ever liked Western films?' she asks you.

If you exit first, go to 58. If Martha exits first, go to 89.

47 'Actually Lieutenant, we weren't exactly travelling with a regular wagon train,' the Doctor confesses. He slips an arm around the man and pulls out his psychic paper again. 'Take another look at my papers,' he suggests.

'Office of the President!' exclaims the man in some surprise.

'Ssh!' the Doctor urges him. 'We're operating undercover.'

The Lieutenant doesn't seem to understand.

'We're here secretly, it's important for our mission that people don't know who we are,' you explain, helpfully.

The Lieutenant scratches his head. 'And what is this secret mission?' he asks.

Martha glances at the Doctor and then steps forward.

'The President is concerned about the level of sickness and the number of deaths on the Western Trails,' says Martha coolly.

'Is that right?' asks the soldier. 'And what is the name of that President? Harrison or Tyler?'

If you answer Harrison, go to 87. If you answer Tyler, go to 98.

48 | The Doctor leads you between a pair of wagons and out of the camp into the open prairie beyond. The sun has all but set now, leaving a deep red glow as it disappears over the horizon. Even with this red glow the stars in the sky seem brighter than you have ever seen before. Martha can see you looking up in amazement.

'No light pollution from street lights and houses here,' she explains, 'so the stars look really bright.'

'So what's that over there?' you ask, pointing across the open plain towards a line of lights in the distance.

The Doctor is staring in the same direction but he is using some night vision glasses to get a better look.

'It's another wagon train,' he tells you.

'Another wagon train?' Martha is surprised. 'Is that likely?'

The Doctor shakes his head. 'Not at all. In fact I'd say it was impossible. That's not just another wagon train. It's an exact copy of this wagon train,' the Doctor tells you.

You take a turn with the night vision glasses to have another look yourself, but as soon as you begin to examine the details of the wagons the whole image starts to fade away.

'What's happening?' you ask.

'I don't know, but I wonder if he does?' asks Martha pointing at a figure lurking out on the prairie, midway between your position and the area where the phantom wagon train was just a few seconds earlier.

'Let's ask him,' suggests the Doctor and starts jogging towards the figure. You and Martha have to run to catch up with him. As you approach the figure you can see that Martha was right — it is a man.

If he is dressed in leather and furs, go to 83. If he is dressed in Native American garb, go to 92.

The alien shape-shifter shrugs and his features begin to blur again. This time the grey mist solidifies into a grey-skinned humanoid with bland, almost unformed, features.

'Sorry,' he tells you, 'but it's very tiring maintaining your forms.'

'You're a Joftli,' says the Doctor. 'I thought your people had all died out!'

'We nearly have,' confesses the alien sadly. 'But there are still a few of us, maybe we can survive if we can just find a new place to be our home.'

'Earth's already occupied,' you tell the alien firmly.

'But we don't want your planet,' the aliens assures you, 'just your gold. We've detected huge deposits in the West of this country.'

'You want to start the Californian Gold Rush early?' states the Doctor,

The alien nods.

If the Doctor tells him that he can't change history, go to 56. If the Doctor has an alternative idea, go to 4.

Standing with the Doctor is a figure, partly hidden in shadows. When he emerges into the light you see that it is another Doctor — a perfect copy of the first right down to the clothes.

'Two of you!' exclaims Martha in surprise.

'No, just the one,' says the Doctor who had been in shadow, 'that one is an impostor.'

The first Doctor sighs heavily. 'Oh, come on,' he says in a tired tone, 'let's not do the old "which is the real me?" routine. Sorry but it's really lame. And unnecessary to boot. We're here to help you.'

The other Doctor gestures urgently at you and Martha. 'Don't listen to that thing. Can't you see — it's some kind of shape-changing monster. You have to kill it.'

The first Doctor just shakes his head sadly. The more manic Doctor shoots him a curious look. 'Too much?' he asks.

The first Doctor nods. 'Just a touch,' he tells his twin.

'The Doctor's not a killer,' Martha tells the deflated-looking second Doctor, moving forward to stand by the real Doctor.

'But I can help you, whoever you are,' the Doctor promises him. 'First you have to explain who you are.'

'Okay,' the impostor tells you, 'but it's a long story...'

'We're in no hurry,' says Martha, 'but please, if you can change your appearance, can you change into something else? One Doctor's more than enough!'

The fake Doctor nods and his features begin to blur and his clothes become indistinct. For a moment there's nothing there but a vaguely human-shaped grey mist and then you're looking at the man you met when you first left the TARDIS.

If that man was a Native American called Running Bear, go to 43. If that man is the wagon train scout named Lieutenant Harvard, go to 9.

'Hey stranger, would you like some stew?' asks the woman.

Even from a few feet away you can smell something delicious cooking in a big pot.

'Yes please,' you answer and a few minutes later you and Martha are sitting down and eating a hearty bowl of tasty stew. The woman has introduced herself as Mrs Robinson and her three children — Patience, Endeavour and Courage — have joined her.

The children are fascinated by your arrival and keep asking you and Martha awkward questions but their mother tells them not to bother you.

Before you can finish your stew the Doctor appears.

'It's getting dark,' he points out, 'we need to be ready.'

You thank Mrs Robinson for the food and get up to follow the Doctor.

If he leads you out of the camp, go to 48.
If he leads you back to the middle of the camp, go to 12.

The woman with the Doctor is wearing a white cotton blouse, a long dark brown heavy skirt and an embroidered apron. She has naturally curly brown hair and lively bright eyes, but her skin is weather-beaten and she looks tired.

'This is Mrs Robinson,' the Doctor tells you, making the introductions.

'I hear you folks have just caught up to us?' says the woman as she shakes your hand.'

You and Martha both look to the Doctor.

'I was explaining how we missed the set-off date,' the Doctor tells you. 'And we've been trying to catch up ever since.'

'I can't believe you've dared to journey alone,' says Mrs Robinson.

'Why's that?' you ask.

The woman shakes her head. 'It's no talk for youngsters,' she states.

> **If the Doctor suggests you and Martha take a look around, go to 94. If the Doctor asks the woman to explain, go to 81.**

You are desperate to find out more about the ghost reports but as soon as you start to ask another question, Martha shakes her head at you. 'Later,' she mouths at you and you button your lip and try to be patient. Putting the children to bed takes ages but eventually all three are asleep and Mrs Robinson retires for the night as well. She leaves you some bedding and shows you a space where you can sleep but all you want is the chance to talk to Martha in private.

You sit by the campfire and Jake makes you some strong coffee. He tells you that he needs to check on the oxen and he leaves you alone. As soon as he is out of sight you turn to Martha.

'What do you think they mean about ghosts?'

'Good question,' says a familiar voice. You spin around and are amazed to see that it is the Doctor.

'Did you have to make us jump like that?' demands Martha.

'Sorry,' the Doctor apologises, 'but I was trying not to cause a disturbance. Come with me.'

He starts to lead you off through the camp.

'Where have you been?' you ask him.

'Oh here and there, talking to people, the usual,' the Doctor says. 'They've all been filling me in on recent events. There's been some odd things happening at night round here.'

'We know,' you tell him. 'Ghosts!'

'Except they're not ghosts, are they Doctor?' adds Martha.

The Doctor nods his head. 'No, they're not ghosts. But something's haunting this wagon train and the strange thing about it is that it's moving with them.'

'Following them?'

But before the Doctor can answer you...

If strange lights flare, go to 6. If a strange sound is heard, go to 32.

Mrs Robinson introduces you to her husband, Jake, and their three children, Patience who is eight, Courage who is six and Endeavour, who is just four years old. The Robinson family are all waiting around a roaring campfire over which a couple of cooking pots are suspended. A tempting aroma reaches your nose. Soon you are sitting down with them and eating a hot and tasty vegetable stew.

'Do you not eat meat?' you ask, a little surprised at the food.

'Not until it's taken us to our new home,' says Jake nodding in the direction of the enclosure containing their oxen.

Martha finishes off her supper, wiping up the last dregs with a hunk of bread.

'I'll sleep well tonight,' she suggests, 'all this exercise, and fresh air…'

The children exchange nervous looks.

'What's wrong?' asks Martha.

If Patience answers, go to 3. If Jake answers, go to 55.

'Don't be starting with any of that ghost nonsense,' a gruff male voice growls suddenly. Mr Robinson has joined your conversation. He is dressed in a similar fashion to the rest of the men — trousers, braces, a loose-fitting shirt, heavy leather boots and an overcoat not dissimilar to the Doctor's. His face is dirty and weather-beaten and, at first glance, he looks a bit frightening, but he has kind eyes.

'But Pa, there are ghosts, you know there are!' Patience dares to continue.

Jake Robinson looks at you directly and speaks earnestly.

'There's a lot of talk like this, and not just from the children, but that's all it is — just talk,' he tells you. 'God-fearin' folk like yourselves don't have anything to worry about.'

If the first person you met was Running Bear, go to 53. If the first person you met was Lieutenant Harvard, go to 25.

'Why not change history?' asks the alien. 'What difference is a few short Earth years going to make?'

'Dabbling in events in an established time stream can be extremely dangerous,' replies the Doctor, intensely. 'You can cause all sorts of damage to the space-time continuum if you don't know what you're doing.'

In response the alien produces a weapon from under a blanket.

'Sorry,' he says, 'but I can't let you stop me.'

'I already have,' states the Doctor with a quiet confidence.

'What do you mean?' stutters the alien, now less sure of himself.

'Before I left my TARDIS I established a dampening field. Any products of high technology won't work now. Even if you get that gold you're not going anywhere.'

'Prove it,' the alien says, defiantly.

The Doctor produces his sonic screwdriver and runs it over the end of the alien's laser weapon. 'Completely dead,' he announces. 'Try it.'

The alien pulls the trigger and nothing happens. The alien's strange droopy features seem to sag even more. 'What am I going to do?' he asks.

The Doctor smiles. 'Leave these people alone, leave history alone and let me take you where you need to go.'

After a moment or two's consideration the alien gratefully accepts the Doctor's offer.

A short time later you watch as the alien leaves the TARDIS to walk out on his new home. The Doctor closes the doors and bounds up to the control console.

'Just one thing puzzles me,' you say, 'if there was a high-technology dampener in effect, how did your sonic screwdriver work?'

'There was no dampener,' confesses the Doctor, 'and I used the sonic screwdriver to disable the weapon.' He grins. 'Right, that's one passenger returned home, now for you!'

Your adventure in time and space is over.

57 'The phantoms were my idea. I wanted to scare the natives to keep them away from our nightly search,' explains the Native American. 'My name is Korst, and I am a loyal servant of the Royal House of Darmounder. This is Lord Jevart—'

'Of the Astares System!' interrupts the Doctor, delighted. 'I knew it, it was on the tip of my tongue. I never forget a tentacle. So what are you doing this far from home?'

The aliens explain that a rogue scientist on their planet developed a semi-sentient space-time craft but the prototype was unstable and disappeared.

'We've been tracking it ever since,' explains Lord Jevart, 'and now we've finally found it. If we can just shut it down we can finally go home.'

'So where is it?'

If it is in the cave, go to 65. If the creature tells you it is elsewhere, go to 77.

58 You step outside the TARDIS and the first thing you notice is the smell and noise of what appears to be a campsite. Huge fabric-covered wagons are drawn up in a massive circle, inside of which numerous small campfires can be seen. Nearby you can see temporary fences marking off areas in which horses and oxen are being fed. In the middle of the camp, half a dozen wagons of essential stores and supplies are drawn up together and it is in the shadow of one of these that the TARDIS has materialised.

Martha joins you.

'It's a wagon train!' she exclaims. 'This is how America was populated. Settlers drove west in these huge convoys to create new lives for themselves.'

If the Doctor is talking to a man in uniform, go to 20. If the Doctor is talking to one of the female settlers, go to 52.

The Doctor thinks he can see a trail and starts walking towards it.

'Are you sure he went this way?' asks Martha, as the tall grass seems to close in around you.

'Ssh!' the Doctor says urgently, by way of a reply.

'There's no need to be rude!' replies Martha, offended.

'No — listen,' orders the Doctor, his expression serious. You can hear something moving, something heavy, coming towards you. Suddenly Running Bear materialises in front of you, emerging from the grass like a ghost.

'The men from the camp are hunting the buffalo,' he tells you, 'we need to be careful.'

'Are buffalo dangerous?' you ask, curiously.

'If one ran into you it'd be like being hit by a small truck,' the Doctor tells you. 'A truck with horns!' he adds.

Running Bear urges you to follow him.

If it is getting dark, go to 62. If not, go to 39.

There is a sudden flash of intense white light that seems to burn your eyes. You are embarrassed but you find yourself screaming. Martha is standing close to you and grabs you by the shoulders.

'It's okay, I'm here,' she assures you.

'But I can't see,' you tell her. 'I'm blind.'

'Close your eyes, and calm down,' Martha orders you, 'it's just temporary, don't panic.'

You try and do as she suggests and when you next open your eyes, although there are still white spots in your vision, you can now see again.

'Where's the Doctor?' you ask.

Martha wheels around. 'I don't know,' she confesses. 'I was looking after you, I didn't see…'

You realise that the Doctor must have gone after the stranger. You see a trail leading off into the tall grass.

If Martha goes first, go to 8. If you go first, go to 86.

The man standing with the Doctor is dressed in simple animal skins, carries a thin shafted hammer-like axe known as a tomahawk and wears his long black hair in a ponytail. He is clearly a Native American, a member of one of the many tribes of indigenous people displaced by the arrival of the European white man in America.

'This is Running Bear,' the Doctor tells you, 'of the Cheyenne.'

'Have you become separated from the rest of your tribe?' asks the Native American in a deep and resonant voice.

'Our wagon train,' explains the Doctor hurriedly, 'and yes, we did get cut off...'

'There is another train close by. I can take you to their camp,' the man informs you.

'Thank you,' the Doctor tells him.

The Native American nods and begins to move away silently.

If you follow him immediately, go to 11.
If you hesitate, go to 95.

You follow your guide into a valley and suddenly you can see the camp laid out before you. It is an impressive sight — far larger than you had anticipated. The individual wagons have drawn themselves up into a circle to form the camp and, within the perimeter formed by the wagons, a great deal of activity can be seen.

As you get closer you can see more clearly everything that is happening inside the camp: animals are being fed, children are playing games, women are cooking and washing, men are repairing damaged wagons and broken wheels.

It looks as if the settlers have been here for days but the Doctor knows better.

'A day or two at best,' he tells you, 'they're emigrants, remember, on their way to start a new life.'

If your guide is a native, go to 17. If your guide is a soldier, go to 69.

63 You have to brave the unpleasant sensation of the matter transporter to return to Earth and then have to make your way back to the TARDIS.

Once back inside the familiar orange and green cavern that is the control room of the Doctor's space and time machine, the Doctor begins to scurry around the mushroom-shaped console, making adjustments and setting controls.

He flicks a switch to open a communications channel with the lost ship.

'Hold on tight,' he says. 'I'm just fixing a virtual "tow-rope" — and then we're off.'

After a short flight through the time vortex you reach the twenty-eighth century and say your goodbyes to the grateful man you've helped get home.

'My turn to go home now, I guess,' you say a little reluctantly.

'Maybe we don't have to take the most direct route home?' suggests Martha.

The Doctor pulls the lever to begin flight. 'Let's see, shall we?'

THE END.

The Native American grabs hold of the tentacle that is gripping the Doctor and tries to pull it free.

'Let go,' he screams at the creature, as if it might actually understand him. 'I don't think he's an enemy.'

To your surprise the monster does as he is told and drops the Doctor to the rocky floor of the cave.

'He isn't of this planet,' he says, accusingly, pointing a tentacle at the Doctor.

'I know,' says the Doctor's rescuer, 'but he is not a threat, my Lord.'

The Doctor is rubbing his throat. 'That's right,' he assures them both taking a step towards them.

'Now perhaps you wouldn't mind explaining what you are doing here and why you've been using your advanced alien technology to make the locals think they're being haunted by phantoms?'

If the monster begins to explain, go to 23.
If the Native American explains, go to 57.

Deep in the cave you find a small device about the size of an MP3 player.

'Is that it?' you ask, rather surprised.

The Doctor carefully picks it up and starts to examine it. It has a clear plastic shell and thousands of multicoloured lights inside.

'Oh this is neat,' he tells you, 'very, very neat. A real work of art.' He sighs and pulls out his sonic screwdriver, adjusts its setting with his thumb and aims it at the alien device. With a groan-like hum the lights go out. The Doctor tosses it to the Native American.

'All safe now. But no more research in this line please — it's not a technology-for-all.'

The crisis averted, the aliens quickly retrieve their hidden spaceship and set off for home. The Doctor tells you that it's time for you to do the same thing.

You set off for the TARDIS.

THE END

'At last!' exclaims the alien. 'I've located my ship.'

The alien explains that she crash-landed here a few months ago, having bailed out from a damaged spaceship in an emergency escape pod. The spaceship is semi-organic and she knew that it would be able to repair itself given time but she didn't know exactly where it landed. The escape pod had come to Earth on the East Coast of the North American continent.

'I've been using this equipment, which I took from the escape pod, to try and track my ship down,' she explains.

'So what caused all the ghostly lights and noises?' you ask.

'A side effect of the scanning devices you were using to look for your ship,' suggests the Doctor.

The alien nods. 'Can you help me get to my ship?'

If you are with a Huygovan, go to 40. If the alien called itself Lalioah, go to 14.

67 | You black out but only for a few moments. When you open your eyes again you find Martha looking over you. She gives you a quick medical examination to make sure there are no lasting effects from whatever it was that knocked you out.

'Some kind of stun grenade,' she suggests, 'but what's someone from the nineteenth century doing with technology like that?' She helps you to your feet.

'Maybe the Doctor will know?' you suggest.

'Well he's bound to have some ideas,' Martha agrees, 'trouble is, he's disappeared.'

You look around you and see that she is right. Both the stranger and the Doctor have gone.

'Did that bloke take him?' you ask Martha.

'Must have,' she replies. 'We have to find them.'

You begin looking around for clues as to the direction they took.

If you find a trail, go to 27. If you hear something, go to 72.

The children all fall silent and stop their game as you approach.

'It's all right,' you tell them, 'we're not going to hurt you.' You smile at them in a reassuring manner but they continue to look at you with suspicion.

'Guess you don't see too many strangers, do you?' suggests Martha kindly.

One boy, about ten or eleven, takes a brave step forward. 'Beg your pardon, Miss, but are you a ghost?' he asks, in a quavering voice. The other children gather behind him.

'A ghost? Why would you think that?' Martha asks them in return.

Before the boy can answer that, a familiar figure joins you — it's the Doctor.

'No time to play games right now,' he tells you. 'We have phantoms to see!'

If the Doctor leads you out of the camp, go to 48. If the Doctor leads you into the middle of the camp, go to 12.

Lieutenant Harvard takes you directly into the camp. He explains that he is the wagon train's scout and had been checking the terrain that the wagon would be covering tomorrow when he came across you. He asks you to wait near the temporary enclosure that contains the train's many oxen and disappears.

Martha looks around her with a little suspicion. 'Am I going to be taken for a runaway slave?' she asks a little nervously.

The Doctor shakes his head. 'We're not in the South — there are plenty of "free" black people in these parts.'

Lieutenant Harvard returns with a large man in an Army uniform who he introduces as Captain George Hamilton, the elected Captain of this wagon train. The Captain is a large man, with a thick black moustache, but he has friendly eyes and a firm, welcoming handshake.

'I hear you got separated from your train and your wagon,' he says to the Doctor.

'That's us — unlucky travellers, I guess,' the Doctor replies brightly, 'but we're not the only ones with problems are we?'

'What makes you say that?' the Captain responds suspiciously.

The Doctor takes a look around. 'How long have you been here?' he asks. 'Two, three days — that's a long stay in one place for travellers hurrying to a new life.'

'You're a very clever man,' comments the Captain.

'Oh, I'm a genius, but I wish people wouldn't bang on about it,' complains the Doctor. 'Tell me what's been happening, I may be able to help.'

The Captain suggests that he gets some hospitality organised for you and Martha first. A friendly-looking woman called Mrs Robinson is asked to take you in; the Doctor tells you he'll join you later.

If Mrs Robinson offers you a meal, go to 30. If you want to sleep, go to 88.

70 The Doctor checks over the spaceship's engines with the sonic screwdriver and discovers that there is enough residual time energy to create a one-way time jump. You return to Earth in the matter transporter and watch from the ground as a star in the night sky suddenly flashes bright and disappears.

'There he goes,' announces the Doctor, 'and now it's our turn. Back to the TARDIS…'

Soon you are back inside the familiar cavern-like control room of the Doctor's space/time craft. You realise that it is your turn to go home. You thank the Doctor for taking you on an adventure.

He smiles at you. 'You didn't do too bad for a first timer,' he tells you, 'you never know, perhaps we can take another trip some time.'

'Yes, please,' you tell him enthusiastically.

'But not today,' he says firmly and sets the controls for Earth in the twenty-first century.

THE END

Suddenly the scout has his weapon in his hand again and takes aim at the alien.

'No!' screams the Doctor. You realise with a sudden cold fear that you are the only person who is near enough to do anything about it.

Everything seems to happen in slow motion. You see the scout's fingers reaching to pull the trigger and, at the same moment feel yourself hurling yourself forwards. As you leap through the air you twist and aim your shoulder at the centre of the scout's back. His finger begins to squeeze the trigger but before it can complete the action you make contact. And now everything suddenly snaps back into normal speed. In an instant the scout is sent flying, his weapon flies out of his hand and the Doctor catches it.

After that everything happens very fast. The alien that had disguised itself as a Native American is able to explain the truth — he was the hunter not the fugitive. He is a Galactic Law Enforcement Officer sent to Earth to recapture a dangerous escaped prisoner — the scout. 'The Cheyenne Tribe took me in while I tracked him down,' he explains, placing his captive into a stasis tube.

A little while later you watch as the alien launches into the sky and then suddenly disappears into hyperspace in a flash of light.

The Doctor turns to you address you.

'Time to get you home now,' he says.

'But what about the ghost wagon train that we saw?'

'Some kind of freak side effect of the alien technology that guy was using to track his quarry?' guesses Martha.

'Either that or it was just something weird and supernatural!' replies the Doctor.

Soon you are back in the TARDIS and on your way home — your adventure is over.

THE END

You think you have heard something. 'Ssh!' you say, and put a finger to your lips.

You and Martha listen, straining your ears. It's faint and hard to be sure of, but there is a distant sound of movement, of grass being pushed aside and something moving swiftly but carefully away.

'That direction,' you announce confidently and set off. Martha hurries to join you.

You follow the sounds through the long grass, away from the wagon train. After a while the grass begins to get shorter and less dense and the ground becomes more rocky and distinctly less flat.

'We've reached the hills,' Martha comments.

Finally you reach the edge of the prairie grass and stop so suddenly Martha almost walks into you.

If the man who took the Doctor was a Native American, go to 85. If the man who took the Doctor was a scout, go to 42.

73 The Doctor is standing in the rear compartment, which is completely out of keeping with the rest of wagon. It is an Aladdin's cave of strange technological devices, all generating the background electronic hum.

The Doctor is examining some of the machines, his dark-rimmed glasses perched on his face as he studies the intricate technology.

'Interesting stuff,' he mutters.

'What is it?' you ask. 'Is this what's been causing the strange phenomena?'

'Trouble is, it asks as many questions as it answers,' the Doctor replies.

'Should we try and shut it down?' asks Martha, practical as ever.

'I'm really not sure,' confesses the Doctor after a moment, 'until we know exactly what it is and why it's here we probably shouldn't touch it at all.'

'I would appreciate that,' says a new voice.

If the new arrival is a woman, go to 79.
If it is a child, go to 36.

Martha steps forward again to answer. 'We're not actually travelling with a full wagon train — we're travelling alone.'

'Alone! Through these territories? That's madness even for homesteaders,' replies the Lieutenant in some surprise.

The Doctor slips a hand into his coat pocket and produces his psychic paper. 'Actually, we're not exactly homesteaders,' he tells the Lieutenant. 'Take a look at this,' he suggests, showing him the blank paper.

The Lieutenant's expression changes as he 'reads' the non-existent words. 'Office of the President?'

The Doctor nods. 'We're agents of the President, conducting a secret mission concerning the security and, er, health issues of the Western Expansion.'

The Lieutenant fixes him with a suspicious look. 'And what is the name of the president who dispatched you on this mission?' he asks.

The Doctor looks blank. What is the right answer?

If you answer Tyler, go to 98. If you answer Harrison, go to 87.

75 A sudden thought strikes you. 'This is our Earth isn't it? Not some parallel world?'

'I think it's our past,' Martha tells you. 'The American West sometime around the middle of the nineteenth century,' she adds.

The Doctor beams. 'Martha Jones — time traveller and historian!'

Martha fixes him with a look and he raises his hands. 'Only joking. But you are doing very well. We're sometime in the early 1840s — the time of the Great Migration.'

'Wagon trains across the prairies and all that?' asks Martha.

'Very good,' says the Doctor, impressed at her historical knowledge.

'Something I have to thank my brother for — Leo went through a big cowboy phase growing up and I saw a lot of Westerns...' Martha explains.

Suddenly Running Bear reappears. 'The camp is about a mile from here,' he tells you.

If it is getting dark, go to 62. If it is still light, go to 39.

76 The scout explains that your quarry will have gone to ground with the local Cheyenne tribe. He leads you out to a strange rock formation and lights a signal fire. He uses a blanket to send a message with smoke signals.

'Now we wait,' he tells you. While you wait he explains what is really going on, telling you that the man you saw is really an alien, a prisoner who escaped.

'Using some kind of portable image manipulator to make himself look human?' suggests the Doctor. 'Like you are?'

The scout is clearly surprised.

'It's very good,' explains the Doctor, 'good enough for human eyes, that is.'

'How long 'til someone answers us?' you ask. The scout tells you that they'll come in person. Suddenly figures appear from all sides. The Cheyenne have you surrounded.

If the Doctor speaks, go to 91. If the scout speaks, go to 28.

77 The aliens lead you back to the woods you first landed in. Here, just 100 or so metres from where the TARDIS landed, you find the missing alien device. It's a small cricket ball-shaped clear plastic sphere, filled with tiny multicoloured lights.

'Talk about looking for a needle in a haystack!' comments Martha.

You pick up the device and the Doctor pops his glasses on and takes a close look.

'Beautiful,' he whispers, and then adds, 'hold it steady for me.'

He gives it a quick blast with the sonic screwdriver and the lights all fade. He plucks it from your hand and tosses it to the humanoid alien.

'Don't let anyone else try this again,' he says sternly, 'this technology is not for you.'

You realise that the adventure is over — it's time to go home. The Doctor leads the way back to the TARDIS.

THE END

You run to check that Martha is OK. 'I'm fine,' she insists, 'don't worry about me. Find the Doctor!'

You do as you are told and hurry in the footsteps of the Native American. Your eyes soon adjust to the blue-tinged darkness. You can see the Doctor being held in the tentacles of what can only be described as a hideous monster. The creature is a huge mass of fat surrounded by tentacles of various thicknesses and lengths. The blue light that fills the rocky chamber seems to be coming from the creature itself and it pulses in time with the thing's heartbeat.

The monster is such an incredible sight that at first you fail to see where the Native American got to but then you spot him.

If the Native American speaks to the monster, go to 84. If he is trying to pull the Doctor clear, go to 64.

You turn around and see that you've been joined by one of the female members of the wagon train community, but when she removes her hat you realise that you may have made a mistake. Although humanoid, her features are subtly alien — little details like delicately pointed ears and flaring eyebrows suggest that she's not a native of this planet.

'I presume this is all yours,' the Doctor says calmly, not at all surprised by the appearance of the new arrival.

'Of course,' the alien woman says, stepping between you to check a display, 'my name is Lalioah.'

The Doctor introduces you all and then asks Lalioah what she is looking for.

The alien looks surprised. 'You recognise what my equipment is for?'

'Call it an educated guess,' says the Doctor, 'so what's the hunt for?'

If she answers you, go to 18. If an alarm starts to sound, go to 66.

80 The wagon train scout runs past you into the mouth of the cave. Martha flashes you a look and then hurries after him. Taking their lead, you follow them into the cave. Inside you find the Doctor lying on the floor and rubbing his head. Martha rushes to his aid.

'It's OK,' the Doctor insists. 'Just a bump on the head. Our friend wasn't playing by the Queensbury Rules.'

'What are you on about?' asks Martha, confused.

The Doctor gets to his feet. 'Rules of boxing,' he explains. He takes in the presence of the scout. 'I take it you're looking for our friend, too? I fear there must be a rear entrance to this cave.'

'He'll be long gone,' announces the scout.

'Do you know where?'

The scout nods.

If the scout leads you to a Native American village, go to 34. If he leads you further into the hills, go to 76.

'Please, don't worry about my companions,' the Doctor insists, 'they've seen all sorts of amazing things.'

The woman looks unconvinced. 'I doubt they've seen anything like we've been seeing. Every night since we set off it's been the same.'

'Why don't you tell us all about it?' suggests the Doctor.

'The first couple of nights just a few folk saw it and they didn't like to say what they'd seen,' explains Mrs Robinson, 'but then the rumours began to spread. Now I don't know many folk who ain't seen it.'

'But what exactly are they seeing?' you ask.

The woman glances in the direction of the setting sun.

'You can see for yourself shortly,' she tells you and advises you on how to get the best view.

If she sends you out of the camp, go to 48. If she sends you to the middle of the camp, go to 12.

Something peculiar happens. You feel as if a bright light is scanning you. You blink and when you open your eyes again you are no longer in the cave but on some kind of spaceship.

'Ah, there you both are,' says a familiar voice. You see the Doctor is here with both the Native American and the scout. 'Matter transporters can be a bit uncomfortable,' he tells you.

'You can say that again,' mutters Martha. 'I think I left my stomach in the cave. Where are we?'

'On this gentleman's spaceship,' says the Doctor, indicating the Native American, 'in orbit.'

'He's an alien?'

'I am human. And I am Cheyenne,' the Native American tells you.

'But from the twenty-eighth century not the nineteenth,' explains the Doctor.

The scout looks on in awe. 'This is madness,' he screams and, pulling a long-bladed knife from his belt, he jumps at the spaceship's owner. There is a flash of energy from a device in the ceiling and he falls to the floor unconscious.

'It's alright,' the Native American assures you, 'he's only stunned. He'll wake up in about twelve hours, unharmed and remembering nothing. The ship is programmed to protect me.'

'So this is a time ship?' asks Martha.

He shakes his head. 'Not by design. I'm an explorer. I found something drifting in deep space, I thought it might be an energy store. Turns out it was some kind of time bomb. I got displaced in time. The phantoms the wagon train saw were my attempts to use the residue time energy to signal for help.'

'And that's where we came in,' says the Doctor. 'Would you like to go home now?'

**If the Doctor uses the TARDIS, go to 63.
If he does something with the spaceship, go to 70.**

83 'Hey there,' the Doctor calls out, 'what were you doing out here just now?

The man regards you all with suspicious eyes.

'I could ask you folks the same question,' he says levelly.

Now he is up close you can see that he is dressed like a frontiersman: buckskin jacket and rough breeches, an animal skin hat which still has the tail attached.

'We're with the wagon train,' Martha tells him confidently, but he doesn't seem impressed.

He looks you all up and down. 'Your clothes look mighty fine for people who've been on the trail a week or two,' he comments. 'You look like you just left the city!'

'Not exactly,' says the Doctor, winking at you.

Suddenly you see that the man has something that looks quite high-tech in his hand.

If it emits a loud alarm, go to 45. If you find yourselves losing consciousness, go to 67.

84 | 'My Lord, stop, please, release him,' screams the Native American, suddenly leaping forward and putting a hand on the tentacle that is holding the Doctor. To your surprise the monster seems to listen to him. Suddenly the tentacle holding the Doctor relaxes and he tumbles to the floor.

'Ouch!' he mutters and then adds, 'thanks.'

You help him get to his feet.

The monster is still quivering and the pulses of blue light are more frequent. You realise that the creature is actually frightened.

'He's not human,' he says in a nervous voice, waving a shaking tentacle in the Doctor's direction.

'But he's not hostile,' insists the Native American.

'That's me,' says the Doctor, smiling broadly, 'mostly harmless. Right,' he continues, 'now we're all mates perhaps you can explain what's going on?'

If the monster begins to explain, go to 23.
If the Native American explains, go to 57.

In front of you there is the mouth of a cave and, from within, an unnatural blue light. You and Martha exchange a look. Martha nods at you to move closer.

You creep up towards the mysterious cave. As you get nearer you can hear a hum of electronic equipment. You can also hear voices, one of which is the Doctor's.

'Oh, now, this is impressive,' you hear him saying.

'He must be in there with the Native American,' Martha whispers to you.

'Should we go inside?' you ask her.

Martha considers for a moment. 'Let's just wait and listen,' she suggests.

'Please, leave me alone,' says the native in his deep and resonant voice. 'Forget all you have seen and go away.'

'Forget all this?!' says the Doctor, incredulously. 'How would I do that? How can I just forget that I've seen a Martian Sonic Grenade or a Quad-Dimensional Radio or a Mark Three Time Wave Generator?'

'You recognise these things? Who are you?' demands the Native American.

'I'm the Doctor,' says the Doctor, 'but, more to the point, who are you?'

You feel something prod you in the back and someone leans in between you and Martha. 'Step back from the cave,' whispers a deep growling voice. 'Both of you.'

You and Martha do as you are asked. 'Turn around,' says the voice. Slowly you turn to face the newcomer and are surprised to see that it appears to be a frontiersman, complete with Davy Crockett-style raccoon skin hat.

'Who are you?' asks Martha.

'Name's Nathaniel McDermott,' he tells you, 'scout for the wagon train and I'm looking for the local who's been poaching our cattle.'

**If the scout goes into the cave, go to 80.
If there is an explosion from inside the cave, go to 5.**

The trail is subtle but it is there — broken and bent grass shows the way. You move as quickly as you can, Martha is right behind you. A sudden worry pops into your head.

'Martha, is there any chance of snakes in this area?' you ask nervously.

Martha hesitates just a moment too long before answering. 'Probably not,' she says, but you're not sure whether to believe her or not.

'To be honest I'm more worried about that guy who attacked us walking about with high-technology like that,' Martha confesses.

'Maybe that's why the Doctor took off in pursuit and just left us,' you suggest.

'Yes, I'm sure it is,' says Martha, but again with a slight hesitation before her answer.

You reach rocky outcrops on a hill.

If you were attacked by a Native American, go to 85. If you were not attacked by a Native American, go to 42.

Martha looks to the Doctor for a clue but he is deep in thought and no help. You decide to answer the question.

'President Harrison,' you say firmly.

'President William Henry Harrison?' he asks again, his voice giving no clue as to whether you've given the right answer.

'Yeah — him,' you say, with a confidence that you don't really feel.

The man looks triumphant. 'So you were sent on this mission by a dead president were you?' he asks sarcastically.

'Of course not,' the Doctor interrupts, 'but you can't expect our young friend here to be up to date with matters like that. The President who dispatched us to these wild parts is President John Tyler of course, tenth president of these United States.'

'His Accidency!' mutters the Lieutenant a little disdainfully.

If you would like to know what he means, go to 37. If not, go to 15.

Mrs Robinson takes you to her wagon, telling you about her family.

'My eldest — Patience — is eight,' she tells you. Then there's Courage, she's six and little Endeavour, he's just four.'

'Why the name Patience?' asks Martha, curious.

'One of the great virtues, isn't it? And Jake and I had to be patient before she came along. Our first child wasn't very healthy and God took her early.'

'I'm sorry,' Martha says.

Mrs Robinson shrugs. 'God moves in mysterious ways,' she tells you. 'Maybe that's why He's testing us again now.'

'Testing you how?' Martha asks.

'Ah, here we are,' announces Mrs Robinson as you reach the wagon and meet the children.

'So what did you mean about being tested?' Martha asks again.

If Patience answers you, go to 3. If a male voice interrupts your conversation, go to 55.

Martha slips out through the doors. 'Wow!' you hear her voice float back to you. 'You have to see this.'

Quickly you go outside, closing the doors behind you.

You see that the TARDIS has materialised amongst five or six massive canvas-covered wagons. Moving between them you join Martha in the open and can see that there are more of the wagons forming a huge circle. Inside this perimeter you can see a number of small campfires and the smell of cooking fills the air.

'It's a wagon train,' Martha tells you. 'Settlers en route to a new life in the West travelled together in these long trains for safety.'

'Where's the Doctor?' you ask.

'Over there,' Martha answers, waving her arm.

If the Doctor is talking to a man in uniform, go to 20. If the Doctor is talking to one of the female settlers, go to 52.

The scout disappears into the rocky hills but Martha hesitates.

'I don't know if we should trust him,' she says.

'We don't have to believe everything he says,' you point out, 'but he clearly knows more about this terrain than we do. If there is another entrance to the caves I think he can take us there.'

Martha considers this a moment and then nods and you set off in pursuit of the scout.

After a short while you catch up with him at the top of a ridge.

'There,' he says pointing towards a tiny crack in another rock face.

'But are they still inside?' asks Martha.

'Let's go and see,' you suggest. The scout nods and disappears into the blackness. You and Martha hurry down to the cave mouth.

If you follow Martha into the dark, go to 82. If you suggest you should go first, go to 44.

91 The Doctor holds his hands up. 'Greetings. Please convey my regards to your chief, Red Wolf. Tell him that Star Walker is here.'

You and Martha are looking at him open-mouthed. The Doctor grins. 'Oh yes, I get around you know. I was here three or four lifetimes ago.'

Before long the Native American chief, wearing a huge headdress of colourful feathers has joined you and is in earnest discussion with his old friend 'Star Walker'. Moments later the mysterious Native American that the scout was hunting is brought before you. The Doctor points his sonic screwdriver at him, disabling his disguise generator. The air ripples and the creature is revealed in its true form. It is a green-skinned humanoid with six-fingered hands.

'Please,' he insists, 'you've got this wrong!'

If the Doctor allows him to speak, go to 19.
If the scout tries to shoot him, go to 71.

The Native American stands his ground as you approach, watching you with dark eyes. He is dressed like every Native American you've ever seen in an old Western.

'I am called Eagle Claw,' he tells you. 'You stand on the sacred lands of the Cheyenne.'

'We are travellers, passing through. We mean you no harm,' the Doctor assures him.

'You hunt and kill our animals, take our land,' Eagle Claw says, 'and yet you say you do no harm?'

'Look we're not really with them,' Martha butts in, waving in the direction of the wagon train.

Meanwhile you are watching the man carefully and you notice his hand reaching for something hanging from his belt. A knife? An axe? No, instead he grabs something that looks, impossibly, like a mobile phone.

If it causes a flash of light, go to 60. If you find yourselves losing consciousness, go to 67.

'Okay,' Martha tells the Native American after a few moments consideration, 'go and help our friend. But please, be careful.'

'He will not come to any harm,' the local man tells you solemnly, 'you have my word as a warrior of the Cheyenne people.'

He begins to move towards the cave. He moves like an animal, swiftly but silently, seeming to blend in with the dark shadows cast by the rocks in the pulsing blue light from within the cave.

Without making a single sound, he is soon at the cave mouth itself. For a moment you and Martha can see him as a black shape at the lip of the cave and then he is gone.

Suddenly there is an explosion from within the cave.

Your guide runs inside and you and Martha follow.

If Martha goes first, go to 82. If you go first, go to 44.

You are surprised when the Doctor agrees with Mrs Robinson. 'Of course, you're right,' he says. 'No need to give my friends here nightmares, eh?'

The woman nods, her face grim. 'Nightmares is the right word for it, believe you me. Take my advice,' she adds looking directly at you and Martha, 'when night falls go inside your wagon and stay there 'til dawn, no matter what you hear.'

'Why don't you and Martha take a look around?' suggests the Doctor. 'Get the lay of the land before it gets dark.'

You're not at all happy to be dismissed like this but Martha gently puts a hand on your arm and leads you away.

'Let's see what we can find out,' she suggests.

You come across some children playing.

If one of them mentions a ghost train, go to 7. If they fall silent when they see you, go to 68.

95 The Native American quickly disappears through the trees and out into a sea of prairie grass, which stretches for miles.

'Should we trust him?' you ask the Doctor in a quiet voice.

'I don't see why not,' he tells you.

'But I thought the Indians—'

'Native Americans,' the Doctor corrects you.

'Sorry, but I thought the Native Americans were hostile and dangerous. Don't they get kicked off their traditional lands by the new colonists spreading out across America?'

The Doctor looks sad. 'Well yes, that's true but the real story is more complicated.'

Martha interrupts with a more urgent concern. 'Well if we're going to trust him we'd better get a move on…'

You take some steps in the direction your guide took but he has completely disappeared.

**If you think you can see a trail, go to 59.
If you decide to wait where you are, go to 75.**

Moving with speed and stealth the scout leads you further into the hills. You and Martha find it difficult to keep up, as the terrain is increasingly difficult but you are determined to find the Doctor.

Eventually you see another rock face decorated with cracks and overhangs. At the base of the rock is a dark hole. As you get closer, you can see that it is a narrow cave mouth.

'How long since the explosion?' you gasp, breathlessly.

'About half an hour,' suggests Martha.

'So have we got here in time or are they already out?' you ask.

'Only one way to find out,' says the scout dashing forwards into the darkness.

You and Martha exchange a look. 'He's right, let's go and take a look,' says Martha.

If you follow Martha into the dark, go to 82. If you suggest you should go first, go to 44.

'Yes,' says the Doctor, confidently. 'The Joftli was using remote control devices to scan for gold and to maintain contact with his hidden spaceship but all his remotes were on pan-dimensional frequencies…'

'So the strange lights and odd noises were what? Feedback?' asks Martha.

'Well it's a bit more complicated than that,' the Doctor begins but Martha cuts through, giving you a wink as she speaks.

'So that's a "yes, Martha, feedback, very well put" is it?'

'Do I really have to keep telling you how clever you are?' teases the Doctor, grinning.

'Isn't that my line?' laughs Martha in return.

'Right,' says the Doctor, 'let's get you back home.'

'Doctor?' Martha's tone makes him look up and he sees your sad expression.

'OK, maybe you can come for another trip soon,' he promises you as the TARDIS lands, 'but right now… your adventure in time and space is over.'

THE END

The silence threatens to last for eternity. The Doctor seems unsure how to answer the question.

'I ask you again, what is the name of the President you claim to be working for?' the Lieutenant repeats his question and this time there is no hiding the threat lurking underneath his words. Martha and you look to the Doctor but he still seems to be racking his brain. Finally you can take the tension no longer. You realise that you've a one in two chance of guessing right.

'John Tyler,' you shout out. The Lieutenant nods.

The Doctor suddenly grins. 'Tenth President of the United States.'

'I don't remember hearing about that one,' mutters Martha.

'He was quite controversial in his time,' the Doctor tells you.

'He's just the Acting President — the Accidency,' adds the Lieutenant.

If you want to hear more about President Tyler, go to 37. If not, go to 15.

Step into a world of wonder and mystery with Sarah Jane and her gang in:

And don't miss these other exciting adventures with the Doctor!